MARC BROWN
ARTHUR'S CHRISTMAS

Piccadilly Press : London

First published in the USA by Little Brown and Co.
An Atlantic/Little Brown Book

British Library Cataloguing in Publication Data
Brown, Marc
   Arthur's Christmas
   I. Title
   813′.54[J]   PZ7
ISBN 0-946826-13-7
Typeset by V & M Graphics Ltd, Aylesbury, Bucks
Printed and bound by Colourcraft Ltd. Hong Kong
For the publishers Piccadilly Press, 64 Greenfield
Gardens, London NW2 1HY, 1985

For my Grandma Thora,
who taught me about giving

Arthur and Diane Winifred had been in the chemist for a long time. "For heaven's sake," Diane Winifred said. "This store is full of presents. Pick one and let's go!"

"It has to be just right," said Arthur. "I want Santa to like it."

"Well, hurry up," said Diane Winifred. "I want to get home and see if Grandma's there and how many presents she brought me."

At home, Diane Winifred added ten more things she wanted to her Christmas list and copied it over in red pencil. Arthur and Diane Winifred cheered when they heard the car in the driveway. "Grandma, are there presents in there for me?" asked Diane Winifred.

"Grandma, do you think Santa would like new mittens or gloves?" asked Arthur.
"Whatever happened to, 'Hello, I'm glad to see you'?" asked Grandma Thora.

GOOD DOG

After dinner, everyone relaxed. "Look," said
Diane Winifred, "I teached Killer a trick."
"Taught," said Grandma. "You taught Killer a
trick." But Diane Winifred didn't hear. She had
seen something on television to add to her list.
"Arthur, what's the matter?" asked Grandma.
"I haven't found the right gift for Santa," said
Arthur.
"Only two shopping days left," reminded Diane
Winifred.

The next day, Arthur, Diane Winifred, and their friends went shopping. Killer went too. Arthur searched the entire store and still couldn't find the perfect gift for Santa. "What's the big problem?" asked Diane Winifred. "I can see a hundred things I want. Let's go and tell Santa."

"Santa, what would you like for Christmas?" asked Arthur.
"Ho, ho, ho, "laughed Santa. "You just leave the giving to me."
Diane Winifred had her picture taken patting Santa's tummy.

Buster was next.

"Santa, be careful coming down the chimney at our house. My parents always forget to put out the fire."

"Ho, ho, ho," said Santa. "Don't worry. I'll use the front door."

Then it was Francine's turn.

"Have you been a good little girl?" asked Santa.

"Oh, yes," smiled Francine. "I'm always good."

"Always?" asked Santa.

Afterwards, Buster treated them all to ice cream. Arthur could hardly finish his milk shake. He had only one more shopping day.

"Look!" said Francine. "Santa eats ice cream!"

"I'll have a banana split with six scoops of bubble gum ice cream," said Santa.

"With double hot fudge, whipped cream, and nuts."

"I'll say he eats ice cream," said Diane Winifred.

15

At home, Arthur asked his family for help.
"How about a nice colourful tie?" said Father

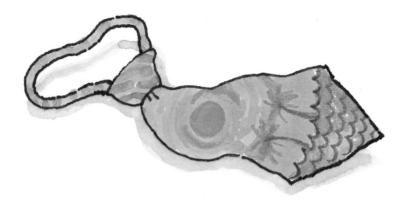

"After-shave is always a good gift," said
Mother.

"I bet Santa could use some toasty-warm long
Johns," said Grandma.

"Arthur, you're taking this shopping too seriously," said Diane Winifred. "Just do what I do. Get everyone the same thing."

That afternoon, everyone was getting ready to
go carol singing.
But Arthur didn't have time for Christmas
carols. Time was running out.
"Please come along," begged Diane Winifred.
"I'll be the only kid. and besides, Mrs. Tibble
always gives us a present and hot chocolate."

Arthur went window shopping instead, hoping that would give him an idea for Santa's present. Santa was Ho-ho-ho-ing and drinking a diet coke at the car wash.

Moments later Santa was at the Golden Chopstick eating subgum chow goo.

Santa must have run to the deli at the corner of North Street. The waitress shouted Santa's order to the cook.

"Catch a fish, hit it with rye, and put a pair of shoes on it!"

"Santa sure eats a lot," thought Arthur.

Finally Arthur went home.

He hadn't seen a single thing in any of the store windows he thought Santa would like.

Santa was on TV eating Papa Piper's pickled peppers.

"That's it!" said Arthur.

He started making his list.

Arthur counted his money.

"Diane Winifred," he said in his sweetest voice.

"Okay, how much do you need?" asked Diane Winifred. "But only if you promise to stop being such a grouch."

24

The next morning, Arthur gave Diane Winifred
half of his list. He took the other half.

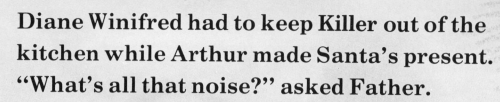

Diane Winifred had to keep Killer out of the kitchen while Arthur made Santa's present.

"What's all that noise?" asked Father.

"Arthur is making a mess," reported Diane Winifred.

The kitchen door opened, and Arthur sneezed.

"Mum, how many cups of pepper in pickled peppers," he asked.

"Maybe I should help," said Mother.

"No, please," said Arthur. "I want to make Santa's present myself. Just tell me how many sticks of gum in subgum chow goo?"

"Poor Santa," said Diana Winifred.

Hours later, Arthur whistled while he set the table for Santa.

"What's that?" asked Father.

"Pickled peppers, a hot fudge sundae on bubble gum ice cream, and subgum chow goo. I sort of combined Santa's favourite foods," Arthur explained.

"What's that big lumpy thing that's moving?" asked Grandma.

"A pizza," said Arthur. "With everything on it."

"If you want Santa to come, you'd better go to bed," said Mother.

"If you want Santa to come," thought Diane Winifred, "we'd better do something about that food."

29

Diane Winifred couldn't fall asleep. "I have to do something," she thought. "Poor Arthur worked so hard. But if Santa gets one whiff of Arthur's present, he'll never set foot in the dining room - much less eat any of it." Careful to miss the squeaky step, Diane Winifred tiptoed downstairs in the dark.

The next morning,
Arthur was the first one up.
"Santa ate it all!" he cried.
"And he left a note!"